KU-733-255

Class No. ___J5-8.___ Acc No. C/230980

Author: Graves, S.   Loc: 5 JUN 2008

**LEABHARLANN
CHONDAE AN CHABHAIN**

6 FEB 2012

1. **This book may be kept three weeks. It is to be returned on / before the last date stamped below.**
2. **A fine of 25c will be charged for every week or part of week a book is overdue.**

(Code 23)

19 SEP 2012

Cavan County Library
Withdrawn Stock

Peg Leg

Practising CVC words plus
phonemes of more than one letter

First published in 2007 by
Franklin Watts
338 Euston Road
London
NW1 3BH

Franklin Watts Australia
Hachette Children's Books
Level 17/207 Kent Street
Sydney
NSW 2000

Text © Sue Graves 2007
Illustration © Martin Remphry 2007

The rights of Sue Graves to be identified as the author
and Martin Remphry as the illustrator of this Work have
been asserted in accordance with the Copyright, Designs
and Patents Act, 1988.

All rights reserved. No part of this publication may be
reproduced, stored in a retrieval system, or transmitted
in any form or by any means, electronic, mechanical,
photocopy, recording or otherwise, without the prior
written permission of the copyright owner.

A CIP catalogue record for this book is available
from the British Library.

ISBN: 978 0 7496 7124 2 (hbk)
ISBN: 978 0 7496 7310 9 (pbk)

Series Editor: Jackie Hamley
Series Advisors: Dr Barrie Wade, Dr Hilary Minns
Series Designer: Peter Scoulding

Printed in China

Franklin Watts is a division of
Hachette Children's Books.

Peg Leg

by
Sue Graves

Illustrated by
Martin Remphry

W
FRANKLIN WATTS
LONDON•SYDNEY

Sue Graves
"I'm not very good at reading maps either. I wonder if Peg Leg's parrot would help me?"

Martin Remphry
"I've always wanted to find some buried treasure, but no luck yet. I will just have to keep on digging!"

CAVAN COUNTY LIBRARY
ACC No. C/230980
CLASS No. J 5·8
INVOICE NO 7834 IES
PRICE €9.01

Peg Leg hid a pot of cash.

CAVAN C
LIBRARY

5

Peg Leg had a map.
"Dig, Jim! Dig!"

But Jim did not dig up
cash. Jim got a shell.

9

"Dig, Jim! Dig!"

11

But Jim did not dig up
cash. Jim got a dish.

13

15

But Jim did not dig up
cash. Jim got a fish.

17

Then Peg Leg got mad.

19

"Dig, Jim! Dig!"
Jim got a pot.

The pot had a lid.
Pop!

Cash!

CAPAN COUNTY LIBRARY

23

Notes for parents and teachers

READING CORNER PHONICS has been structured to provide maximum support for children learning to read through synthetic phonics. The stories are designed for independent reading but may also be used by adults for sharing with young children.

The teaching of early reading through synthetic phonics focuses on the 44 sounds in the English language, and how these sounds correspond to their written form in the 26 letters of the alphabet. Carefully controlled vocabulary makes these books accessible for children at different stages of phonics teaching, progressing from simple CVC (consonant-vowel-consonant) words such as "top" (t-o-p) to trisyllabic words such as "messenger" (mess-en-ger). READING CORNER PHONICS allows children to read words in context, and also provides visual clues and repetition to further support their reading. These books will help develop the all important confidence in the new reader, and encourage a love of reading that will last a lifetime!

If you are reading this book with a child, here are a few tips:

1. Talk about the story before you start reading. Look at the cover and the title. What might the story be about? Why might the child like it?

2. Encourage the child to reread the story, and to retell the story in their own words, using the illustrations to remind them what has happened.

3. Discuss the story and see if the child can relate it to their own experience, or perhaps compare it to another story they know.

4. Give praise! Small mistakes need not always be corrected. If a child is stuck on a word, ask them to try and sound it out and then blend it together again, or model this yourself. For example "wish" w-i-sh "wish".

READING CORNER PHONICS covers two grades of synthetic phonics teaching, with three levels at each grade. Each level has a certain number of words per story, indicated by the number of bars on the spine of the book:

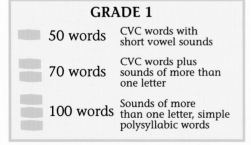

GRADE 1

50 words — CVC words with short vowel sounds

70 words — CVC words plus sounds of more than one letter

100 words — Sounds of more than one letter, simple polysyllabic words

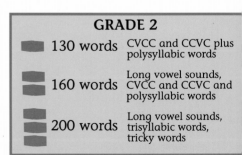

GRADE 2

130 words — CVCC and CCVC plus polysyllabic words

160 words — Long vowel sounds, CVCC and CCVC and polysyllabic words

200 words — Long vowel sounds, trisyllabic words, tricky words